WILL MIA PLAY IT SAFE?

A Book About Trying New Things

JaNay Brown-Wood

Illustrated by **Lorian Tu** *and* **Leo Trinidad**

Charlesbridge

At 123 Sunshine Street, five best friends are always up for playing together.

But the members of the Sunshine Squad—a group of everyday heroes who spread sunshine to others—have no idea a new kid has just moved into their building. And anyone can feel a bit uncertain about trying something new. . . .

Outside their building, Mia, Lucas, Sophie, and Oliver can't decide what to play next.

"We could draw comics," says Oliver, pulling his handy pencil from behind his ear. "I want to show you how to draw this new superhero!"

Mia doesn't think there's any way she could ever draw a picture as super as Oliver can.

"You guys go ahead," she says. "I need to practice my dribbling."

Later Sophie hands everyone a small plastic animal. "Let's play baby animals at the pet shelter," she says. "I just got these new cuties!"

"I'll watch," Mia says. She always feels like she's the worst at make-believe.

"Who's ready to learn a new trick?" Lucas asks the next day, showing off his deck of magic cards.

"That's OK," Mia says. "I need to do a few more drills."

"Count me in!" Oliver shouts.

Everybody seems so comfortable trying new things, Mia thinks. *Not me. What if I get it wrong?*

The next day it's Mia's turn to pick what the squad will do together. She suggests, "Let's play basketball!"

"We knew that's what you would pick," Sophie says.

"Good thing I've got my high-tops on," Oliver says.

"I'm going to play with my cars instead," says Tommy.

Just as they finish picking their teams of two, a new girl walks up.

"I'm sorry," says Mia. "We've already picked teams. It would be uneven if you joined. Maybe next time."

The girl nods and skips off.

When the game gets started, Mia can't stop thinking about the new girl. She wanted to try something new with a bunch of kids she doesn't even know. *That's pretty brave*, Mia thinks.

"Great game!" Mia says.

"Basketball's cool and all, but check this out," Lucas replies, pulling two magic coins from his pocket.

"I'll just keep practicing," Mia says.

"Sometimes it seems like that's the only thing you like to do," Lucas says.

Mia frowns. Other things never seem to come easily to her. But basketball always does. It's what she's good at.

Why would she try something new?

Later, when they are all walking back to their building, Oliver points ahead. "Hey, isn't that the girl from the park?"

"Maybe she lives here now," says Sophie. "I wonder if she likes animals."

"Or cars!" adds Tommy.

Mia doesn't say anything. She is still thinking about what Lucas said.

The next week the gang is back to basketball.
Even Tommy wants to play this time.

As they line up to pick teams, Mia spots
someone next to the swings.

"Hold on one sec," she says. Mia's hands
are a little shaky, and her heart speeds up
as she walks over to the new girl.

"Hi!" she says, finding her voice. "I'm Mia."

"I'm Lillian. But you can call me Lily."

"Do you want to play some basketball? We've got room for one more."

"OK! But you should know that I really don't know how to play, so I'm probably not very good."

"That's OK," Mia says. "Maybe we can teach you."

Game on! It's Mia, Lily, and Lucas against Oliver, Sophie, and Tommy.

"When the ball gets tossed to you, try to grab it with both hands!" Mia calls to Lily.

"Like the ball is a pretty kitty you don't want to drop," adds Sophie.

"OK!" Lily says.

"Next time, bend your knees and then jump up when you shoot," Mia says.

"Yeah, like you're a rocket ship about to blast into space," Tommy says.

"Then let your arm follow through like this!" Mia adds.

"Got it," replies Lily.

By the end of the game, it's all tied up.
"Next point wins," calls Oliver.

Lily dribbles fast and passes the ball to Mia. Mia
catches it, takes a shot, and misses. But Lily
rebounds, shoots, and . . . makes it!

"We win!" Lily shouts.

"Great job!" says Mia. "You're not half bad."

"I got the hang of things—with everyone's help,"
Lily says. "Thanks for giving me a shot, Mia."

Mia can't help but blush a little. "You're welcome."

"What should we do next?" asks Lucas.

"I was going to say play cars, but this one
is missing a wheel," says Tommy.

"Can I see it?" asks Lily. She unzips her fanny pack
and pulls out a tiny toy wheel. The Squad watches
closely as she pops it onto Tommy's car. "Try it now."

Tommy smiles as his toy zooms across the blacktop.

"That was super awesome," says Oliver.

"I always carry tools and spare parts," Lily says. "I like to build things."

"I've never built or fixed anything cool like that," says Mia. *It looks way too hard*, she thinks.

"In my old neighborhood, my friends and I built things all the time," Lily says. "Maybe I can show you, like you showed me how to play basketball!"

"We can build in our fort at Lucas's," says Oliver. "That is, if you want to join our Sunshine Squad."

Lily beams.
"That sounds great."

Lily grabs her special box of little car parts, ramps, and gadgets from her apartment.

The squad—plus their newest member— races to Lucas's apartment!

"I'll just watch," says Mia.

"Don't worry! It's not too hard," says Lily. "Come on, I'll show you. Try that piece right there and push it in like this."

Mia clicks the two pieces into place. "Got it! Now what?"

"Great!" Sophie says. "Now you build something."

"But what?" Mia asks.

"Anything you like!" says Lily.

Mia tries, but the pieces don't fit.

She picks up another until she finds a match.

"Perfect!"
Mia shouts.

As Mia slowly gets the hang of building, it feels pretty fun to keep trying. And it feels even better to have friends willing to help her out, including a cool new one.

That's when Mia turns to Lucas. "You should teach us some of those card tricks next."

Lucas smiles, and—*poof!*—like magic, the whole squad agrees.

Making Friends with a Puppet

The first thing I noticed was her hair. It was black and long and shiny, like my music teacher's piano. I thought she looked like a princess. She stood all alone at the edge of the school playground.

"Who is she?" I asked my teacher. I aimed a nod at the girl.

"She's the new girl in Mrs. McNair's class," my teacher said. "She's from a migrant worker family. They don't speak English—only Spanish."

I didn't know anything about migrant workers, but I did know a few Spanish words. I knew that uno, dos, tres, meant one, two, three. I knew adios meant good-bye. If I could get those words right, I thought, I could talk to that girl.

I walked toward her, my mouth as dry as the playground's sandbox. I stopped a few steps away from her. She looked up at me. I opened my mouth, but the words were all wrong. What kind of conversation is "one, two, three, goodbye"? I turned and ran. For the rest of recess, I watched her from the safety of the tetherball line.

Every day, she stood in the same spot on the edge of the playground, and every day, I tried to think of something to say or do. The easiest thing to do was to pretend I didn't see her, just like all the other kids did. But doing this bothered me.

A couple weeks later, I moped into Mom's bedroom one afternoon. She was making felt puppets for the church bazaar. I picked up the black yarn Mom was using for the puppets' hair. It reminded me of the new girl's shiny hair.

"Mom, can I make a puppet?" I said.

"Sure," Mom said.

I used tan felt for the puppet's skin and long, shiny black yarn for its hair. Mom helped me find two brown buttons for the eyes. That night, I went to sleep with the puppet tucked under my pillow and a plan tucked in my head.

The next day, I could hardly wait until recess. Spelling seemed to take forever. When the bell finally rang, I ran outside with the puppet. I saw the girl standing in her usual spot. I pulled the puppet out of my pocket and slipped it over my hand. I hurried across the playground and sat next to the new girl.

"Hello," said the puppet (in my voice). "Want to play with me?"

I handed her the puppet and helped her slip it on her hand.

At first, the puppet moved without saying anything. Then, it spouted words that danced into my ear. The words made no sense to me, but one word jumped out from the others. "Luisa," the puppet said. "Luisa." She handed the puppet back to me.

"Hello, Luisa. This is Lana," I said, making the puppet point to me. "She wants to be your friend."

We took turns with the puppet for the rest of recess. When I held the puppet, it spoke English, and when Luisa did, it spoke Spanish. The bell rang. Luisa tried to give me the puppet, but I pushed it toward her. "It's for you," I said.

Luisa's smile warmed me inside. It was the kind of smile I knew I'd never forget.

The next day, I ran outside at recess and looked for Luisa. She wasn't there. The next day was the same. She was gone. I found Mrs. McNair refereeing a foursquare game.

"Where's Luisa?" I asked.

"Her family moved again," she said.

"But she just got here," I protested. Mrs. McNair shrugged.

I turned and wandered toward the edge of the playground. I stood in the spot where Luisa used to stand. I was glad she had the puppet. And I was glad I had the memory of Luisa's smile.

—Lana Krumwiede

Story by Lana Krumwiede, *Chicken Soup for the Child's Soul*.
© 2012 Chicken Soup for the Soul, LLC. All rights reserved.

5 Things to Remember When You Try Something New

1. It's OK to feel a little nervous about trying something new. This means you want to get it right. But even if you get it wrong the first few times, that's OK, too. Few of us are really good at everything right away! Trying things more than once can help build skills.

2. It's OK to be nervous about meeting new friends, too. Try inviting someone new to join an activity you enjoy. Then ask what they like to do, and join in. Talking about our interests helps us get to know one another!

3. Recognize when others are trying new things. You can be just as brave as they are.

4. Look for helpers who can give you a hand when you're learning something new.

5. When you try something new, give it your best shot. It's OK if you don't like it, but giving it an honest chance is what counts. Who knows? Trying something new might bring some sunshine to your life!

To you, my one and only Lonie—my best friend since I met you decades ago at Aynesworth Elementary—J. B.-W.

Published by Charlesbridge
9 Galen Street
Watertown, MA 02472
(617) 926-0329
www.charlesbridge.com

Library of Congress Cataloging-in-Publication Data
Names: Brown-Wood, JaNay, author. | Tu, Lorian, illustrator. | Trinidad, Leo, illustrator.
Title: Chicken soup for the soul KIDS: will Mia play it safe?: a book about trying new things / JaNay Brown-Wood, illustrated by Lorian Tu and Leo Trinidad.
Description: Watertown, MA: Charlesbridge, [2022] | Series: Chicken soup for the soul. Kids | Audience: Ages 3–6. | Audience: Grades K–1. |
Summary: "Mia is good at basketball and sticks to playing it even when her friends in the Sunshine Squad like to do other activities; trying new things makes Mia feel anxious about failing—that is, until Lily moves in and inspires Mia to go outside her comfort zone."—Provided by publisher.
Identifiers: LCCN 2021015679 (print) | LCCN 2021015680 (ebook) | ISBN 9781623542795 (hardcover) | ISBN 9781632899521 (ebook)
Subjects: LCSH: Self-confidence—Juvenile fiction. | Anxiety—Juvenile fiction. | Conduct of life—Juvenile fiction. | Friendship—Juvenile fiction. | CYAC: Self-confidence—Fiction. | Conduct of life—Fiction. | Friendship—Fiction.
Classification: LCC PZ7.B81983 Mi 2022 (print) | LCC PZ7.B81983 (ebook) | DDC 813.6 [E]—dc23
LC record available at https://lccn.loc.gov/2021015679
LC ebook record available at https://lccn.loc.gov/2021015680

Printed in China
(hc) 10 9 8 7 6 5 4 3 2 1

Illustrations created digitally
Display type set in Midnight Chalker by Hanoded
Text type set in Oxford by Roger White
Color separations and printing by 1010 Printing International Limited in Huizhou, Guangdong, China
Production supervision by Jennifer Most Delaney
Series design by Kristen Nobles
Book designed by Lilian Rosenstreich